Codefendant

Rachael Reed
©2024

 RACHAEL REED

Chapter 1: Monie's Perfect Life

Monie was living the life most people only dreamed of. At 26, she had everything going for her. A great job at a marketing firm downtown, a loving family that supported her every move, and a circle of friends that kept her grounded. She had no kids, no drama, and had never been in trouble a day in her life. Monie was the definition of a good girl.

Her weekdays were a routine of early morning workouts, long hours at the office, and evenings filled with laughter and wine with her girlfriends. Weekends were for brunches, shopping, and family gatherings. Life was good, simple, and predictable.

But then she met Rico.

Rico was everything Monie's life wasn't—exciting, dangerous, and full of mystery. They crossed paths at a trendy lounge downtown. Monie was out with her girls, celebrating another successful project at work, when Rico strolled in. Tall, dark, and undeniably handsome, he had an air of confidence that was impossible to ignore. His presence commanded the room, and Monie found herself inexplicably drawn to him.

"Yo, what's up beautiful?" Rico said, sliding up next to her at the bar. "Can I buy you a drink?"

Monie, normally cautious around strangers, felt a rush of excitement. "Sure, why not?" she replied, smiling.

Their chemistry was instant and electric. They talked and laughed, the conversation flowing effortlessly. Rico was charming, funny, and attentive. He listened to Monie like she was the only person in the room, making her feel special in a way she hadn't in a long time.

As the night wore on, Monie learned bits and pieces about Rico. He was 32, ran his own business, and had a magnetic charm that made it hard for Monie to look away. He didn't talk much about his work, brushing off her questions with a grin and a change of subject. Monie didn't mind; she was too captivated by his presence to care.

Their relationship moved quickly. Rico swept Monie off her feet, taking her on spontaneous trips, showering her with gifts, and making her feel like the queen she was. Monie's friends and family noticed the change in her, how happy and alive she seemed.

"Girl, you lookin' good," her best friend Keisha said one day over brunch. "Rico must be puttin' it down."

Monie laughed, blushing. "He's amazing, Keisha. I feel like I've finally found someone who gets me."

But not everyone was as charmed by Rico as Monie was. Her brother, Jamal, was suspicious from the start.

"Monie, you know anything 'bout this dude?" Jamal asked one evening. "He seems too good to be true."

"Come on, Jamal. Not everyone's out to get me. Rico's different," Monie insisted.

"Just be careful, sis. Streets talk, and I hear things."

Monie brushed off Jamal's concerns. She was too deep into her love story with Rico to see the red flags. Rico's phone was always buzzing, but he never let her see who was texting. He had a way of disappearing for hours, sometimes days, with vague explanations that didn't quite add up. When she asked, he'd smile, kiss her, and tell her not to worry.

"Baby, I got you. You don't need to stress over nothin," Rico would say, and Monie would believe him.

One night, Monie overheard a conversation Rico was having on the phone. His tone was sharp, and the language was rough. She caught words like "shipment" and "cut," but when he saw her listening, he quickly ended the call.

"Business stuff," he said, brushing it off with a kiss on her forehead. "You don't need to worry 'bout that."

Monie's gut told her something was off, but she ignored it, choosing to believe in the fairytale Rico was selling her. She was too enamored by the passion and excitement he brought into her life to notice the shadows lurking around the edges.

As Monie's perfect life intertwined with Rico's chaotic world, she remained blissfully unaware of the storm brewing on the horizon. The streets had their own rules, and soon enough, Monie would learn just how deep Rico's ties to that life went. But for now, she was caught in the thrill of her newfound love, blind to the dangers that lay ahead.

Chapter 2: Falling for Rico

Monie was head over heels for Rico. The way he showered her with affection and gifts made her feel like the luckiest woman in the world. Every time she opened her eyes, there was something new—a designer bag, diamond earrings, or a surprise weekend getaway. Rico had a way of making her feel special, and Monie was intoxicated by it.

One evening, Rico surprised her with a trip to Miami. "Pack your bags, baby. We flyin' out tonight," he said, a mischievous grin on his face.

"Miami? For real?!" Monie squealed, wrapping her arms around his neck.

"For real," Rico said, kissing her deeply. "I want to treat my queen right."

The trip was everything Monie dreamed of—sun, sand, and luxury. Rico rented a penthouse suite overlooking the ocean, and they spent their days lounging on the beach and their nights dancing under the stars. Monie couldn't believe her luck. She felt like she was living in a fairytale.

But back home, things were different. Monie's friends and family started to voice their concerns more openly.

"Monie, girl, you sure 'bout this Rico dude?" Keisha asked one afternoon over drinks. "He got that too-good-to-be-true vibe, you know?"

"Keisha, you don't understand. Rico's different. He treats me like a queen," Monie replied, rolling her eyes.

"Yeah, but where he gettin' all that money from? Ain't no regular job payin' for trips to Miami and all that bling," Keisha pressed.

"Look, I trust him. He's a businessman," Monie said defensively. "He ain't doin' nothin' wrong."

Her family was even more direct. Jamal, her brother, sat her down one evening. "Monie, I know you grown and can make your own choices, but Rico ain't right. I been hearin' things on the street."

"Jamal, you always thinkin' the worst. Rico's legit. He's just private 'bout his business," Monie argued.

"Just be careful, sis. These streets don't play fair," Jamal warned, his tone serious.

Despite the warnings, Monie brushed off their concerns. She was in love, and nothing was going to ruin that for her. Rico was her everything, and she trusted him completely.

However, as their relationship deepened, Rico's street activities started to become more apparent. There were late-night phone calls that he always took in another room, whispered conversations with shady characters, and frequent disappearances with no explanations.

One night, as they were lying in bed, Rico's phone buzzed. He glanced at the screen and immediately got up. "I gotta take this," he said, heading to the balcony.

Monie lay there, listening to his muffled voice through the glass door. She caught bits and pieces—words like "shipment," "drop," and "watch your back." A knot formed in her stomach, but she quickly pushed the doubts aside. Rico wouldn't put her in danger. He loved her.

The next day, Monie found herself at Rico's place alone. As she tidied up, she stumbled upon a small black bag tucked behind his closet. Curiosity got the best of her, and she opened it to find stacks of cash and small, sealed packages. Her heart raced, but when Rico came home, she didn't say anything.

"Everything good, baby?" he asked, kissing her cheek.

"Yeah, everything's perfect," Monie lied, forcing a smile.

As time went on, the signs became harder to ignore. Rico's temper flared more often, especially when Monie questioned his whereabouts. "Why you always gotta be up in my business?" he snapped one evening.

"Because I care 'bout you, Rico. I'm worried," Monie said softly.

"You don't need to worry 'bout nothin'. I got this," Rico said, brushing off her concerns.

Despite the growing unease, Monie remained in denial. She loved Rico too much to let go, clinging to the hope that everything would work out. She convinced herself that the life they were building was worth the risks.

But deep down, Monie knew something was off. The glamour and excitement were starting to fade, replaced by a gnawing fear that the fairytale she was living might come crashing down. Yet, she pushed those thoughts away, choosing to live in the moment with the man she loved.

As the shadows of Rico's world grew darker, Monie's perfect life began to unravel. She was caught in a web of love and danger, unable to see the full picture of the life she had stepped into. The streets whispered their warnings, but Monie wasn't ready to listen. Not yet.

Chapter 3: The Wake-Up Call

Monie's day started like any other. She was at Rico's place, tidying up while he was out handling business. The sun streamed through the windows, casting a warm glow over the apartment. Monie hummed to herself, lost in thoughts about their future. But as she moved a stack of clothes in Rico's closet, she stumbled upon a heavy duffel bag she hadn't noticed before.

Curiosity piqued, Monie unzipped the bag and her breath caught in her throat. Inside were stacks of cash, neatly bound in rubber bands, and several small packages wrapped tightly in plastic. Her heart pounded in her chest as the realization hit her—Rico was deeper in the game than she had ever imagined.

"Oh my God," she whispered, feeling her world tilt.

Just then, the door clicked open, and Rico walked in. He froze when he saw Monie holding the open bag. His face darkened, a storm brewing in his eyes.

"What the hell you doin'?" he snapped, striding over and yanking the bag from her hands.

"I— I was just cleaning, and I found—" Monie stammered, fear and confusion mingling in her voice.

Rico slammed the bag shut and threw it into the closet. "You ain't supposed to be snoopin' around my stuff, Monie," he growled, his anger barely contained.

"I wasn't snooping, Rico! I was just—" she tried to explain, but he cut her off.

"Just what? Puttin' your nose where it don't belong? You need to stay outta my business," he said, his tone harsh and unforgiving.

Monie felt tears prick at the corners of her eyes. "I thought you said you were done with this shit, Rico. What happened to keeping me safe?"

Rico's expression softened slightly, but his eyes were still hard. "I am keepin' you safe. That's why you don't need to know 'bout this. The less you know, the better."

"How can I feel safe when you're hiding things from me? When I don't know what's going on?" Monie's voice wavered, torn between love and fear.

Rico stepped closer, his tone lowering. "Monie, listen to me. I'm doin' this for us. To build a life for us. You gotta trust me."

"Trust you? How can I trust you when you're lying to me? When you're putting us both in danger?" she shot back, her anger rising to match his.

Rico grabbed her by the shoulders, his grip firm but not painful. "I ain't puttin' you in danger, Monie. I'm keepin' you out of it. I'm protectin' you."

Monie searched his eyes, looking for the man she fell in love with. "But at what cost, Rico? What happens when it all falls apart?"

"It ain't gonna fall apart. I got this under control," he insisted, his voice steady and confident.

Monie shook her head, tears streaming down her face. "I don't know if I can do this, Rico. I'm scared."

Rico pulled her into his arms, holding her tight. "I know, baby. But you gotta trust me. I won't let anything happen to you. I promise."

Monie wanted to believe him, wanted to trust that everything would be okay. But deep down, she knew the truth.

Rico's world was dangerous, and no amount of promises could change that.

As the days went by, Monie found herself living in a constant state of anxiety. Every time Rico left the house, she worried if he would come back. Every unknown number on her phone made her heart race, fearing it was bad news.

She loved Rico deeply, but the fear was growing stronger. She was trapped between her love for him and the undeniable truth of his lifestyle. The streets were unforgiving, and Monie was starting to realize that being with Rico meant living on the edge.

One night, as she lay in bed alone, Monie stared at the ceiling, tears slipping silently down her cheeks. She didn't know what to do, didn't know how to reconcile her love for Rico with the fear that gnawed at her soul.

"I love you, Rico," she whispered into the darkness, knowing he couldn't hear her. "But I'm so scared."

The wake-up call had been harsh, and Monie knew that life with Rico would never be simple. The streets had a hold on him, and by extension, on her. And no matter how much she loved him, she couldn't shake the feeling that things were only going to get worse.

Chapter 4: Trouble on the Horizon

Monie was starting to feel the pressure. The nights were getting colder, the shadows longer. She could feel eyes on her whenever she stepped out. Rico's enemies were taking notice of her, and it was only a matter of time before trouble knocked on her door.

One evening, Monie was leaving the grocery store, juggling bags in her hands when a car slowly rolled up beside her. The window lowered, revealing a menacing face she didn't recognize.

"Yo, you Rico's girl?" the man asked, his voice low and threatening.

Monie's heart skipped a beat. She kept walking, trying to ignore him, but he persisted, trailing her.

"Tell your man we lookin' for him. He can't hide forever," the man sneered before speeding off, leaving Monie shaken and scared.

She rushed home, her hands trembling as she fumbled with her keys. When she finally got inside, she locked the door behind her, leaning against it for support. The fear was becoming too real, too close.

Rico came home later that night, finding Monie pacing the living room. "What's wrong, baby?" he asked, concern etched on his face.

"I was followed today, Rico. Some guy in a car said he's looking for you," Monie replied, her voice trembling.

Rico's expression darkened, his jaw clenching. "What did he look like?"

"Mean. I didn't get a good look, but he knew me. Knew who I was," she said, wrapping her arms around herself.

Rico pulled her into his arms, holding her tightly. "I'm sorry, Monie. I didn't want you to get dragged into this. I'll handle it. You just need to stay inside, keep a low profile."

"But how long can I keep doing this, Rico? I'm scared all the time. I can't live like this," Monie whispered against his chest.

"I know, baby. I know. But I'm doing everything I can to protect you," Rico said, his voice filled with a mix of anger and desperation.

As the days passed, Rico became more paranoid and controlling. He insisted on driving Monie everywhere, not letting her out of his sight. He was constantly on edge, checking his phone, looking over his shoulder. The tension was suffocating.

One night, Monie woke up to find Rico pacing the living room, talking on the phone in hushed tones. She listened from the hallway, her heart sinking as she caught snippets of the conversation.

"We need to move that shit now... No, she don't know nothin'... Just keep it low, man. I got enough problems."

When he finally hung up, Monie stepped into the room. "Rico, what's going on?"

"Just business, baby. Don't worry 'bout it," he said, but his eyes were hard and distant.

"I can't help but worry. You're scaring me, Rico. I don't know who you are anymore," Monie said, her voice breaking.

Rico sighed, rubbing his face with his hands. "I'm doing this for us, Monie. To keep you safe. I need you to trust me."

Monie's frustration boiled over. "How can I trust you when you keep me in the dark? When I'm being threatened because of you?"

Rico's temper flared. "You think I want this? I'm trying to fix it, but you need to let me handle it my way."

Monie's eyes filled with tears. "I love you, Rico, but I'm starting to see the cracks. This life... it's dangerous, and I'm scared we won't make it out."

Rico pulled her into his arms, his grip almost too tight. "We will, Monie. I promise you. I just need time."

But time was running out. The threats were becoming more frequent, the danger more palpable. Monie could see the strain on Rico's face, the worry lines that hadn't been there before. He was losing control, and she was caught in the crossfire.

One afternoon, while Rico was out, Monie received a call from an unknown number. She hesitated before answering, her heart pounding.

"Monie, this is Keisha. You need to get out, girl. People are talking. It's getting bad," her friend warned.

Monie's hands shook as she hung up. The walls were closing in, and she felt trapped in a life she no longer recognized. The love she had for Rico was battling with the fear that gnawed at her every day.

The horizon was darkening, and Monie knew she had to make a decision. She couldn't keep living in denial, couldn't keep ignoring the dangers. The streets were closing in, and the life she once thought was perfect was now crumbling around her.

Monie stared out the window, her mind racing. She had to find a way out, a way to protect herself. The trouble on the horizon was becoming a storm, and she had to weather it before it destroyed everything she held dear.

Chapter 5: The Bust

The morning started like any other. Monie was in the kitchen making coffee when she heard the loud, urgent pounding on the door. Her heart leapt into her throat. Before she could react, the door burst open, and a swarm of federal agents stormed in, guns drawn and shouting commands.

"Hands up! Everyone on the ground!" one agent barked.

Monie froze, her mind racing. Rico emerged from the bedroom, eyes wide with shock and anger. "What the fuck is this?" he shouted.

"Get on the ground, now!" an agent screamed, shoving Rico to the floor and slapping handcuffs on him.

Monie dropped to her knees, her hands shaking. "I didn't do anything," she cried, tears streaming down her face. "I don't know what's going on!"

"Ma'am, stay calm. We need to ask you some questions," another agent said, pulling her up roughly and leading her out of the apartment.

Outside, the street was a scene of chaos. Rico's associates were being rounded up, handcuffed, and shoved into squad cars. Monie saw faces she recognized from late-night visits and hushed conversations. The realization hit her like a punch to the gut—Rico's world was crumbling, and she was caught in the fallout.

At the federal building, Monie was placed in a sterile, cold interrogation room. The minutes felt like hours as she waited, fear gnawing at her insides. Finally, two agents entered, their expressions unreadable.

"Monie Williams," one of them said, sitting down across from her. "We need to talk about your boyfriend, Rico Hernandez."

"I don't know anything," Monie stammered, her voice shaking. "I swear, I don't."

The agent leaned forward, his eyes piercing. "We have evidence that suggests otherwise. You've been living with him, traveling with him, benefiting from his illegal activities. That makes you complicit."

"No, I didn't know! I thought he was a legitimate businessman!" Monie pleaded, tears streaming down her face.

"Whether you knew or not, you're in this now," the agent said coldly. "You can either help us, or you can go down with him. We're prepared to offer you a deal."

Monie's heart pounded in her chest. "What kind of deal?"

"Testify against Rico. Tell us everything you know, and we'll consider reducing your sentence," the agent said, sliding a piece of paper across the table. "Or you can keep quiet and face a ten-year sentence for conspiracy."

Monie's mind spun. Testify against Rico? Betray the man she loved? But the alternative—a decade in prison for something she didn't even understand—was unthinkable. She felt trapped, the walls closing in around her.

"I need to think," she whispered, her voice barely audible.

"You don't have much time," the agent replied, standing up. "We'll be back in an hour. Make your decision."

Alone in the room, Monie's thoughts raced. She thought of her family, her future, everything she'd worked so hard for. But then she thought of Rico, the man who had promised to protect her, the man who had dragged her into this nightmare.

The hour passed in a blur of tears and frantic thoughts. When the agents returned, Monie took a deep breath, her decision made.

"I'll testify," she said, her voice trembling. "But you have to protect me."

The agent nodded, a small, satisfied smile playing on his lips. "You made the right choice, Monie. We'll make sure you're safe."

Monie felt a hollow victory. She had chosen survival over loyalty, but the cost was her soul. As they led her out of the interrogation room, she wondered if she would ever find peace again. The streets had claimed another victim, and Monie's perfect life was shattered beyond repair.

In the days that followed, Monie's life became a whirlwind of legal meetings and preparations for court. The feds kept her in protective custody, away from the prying eyes of the media and Rico's associates. She felt like a prisoner in a gilded cage, trapped by the choices she had been forced to make.

Every night, she lay awake, haunted by memories of Rico and the life they had shared. She had loved him deeply, but now she had to destroy him to save herself. The guilt gnawed at her, but there was no turning back. The path she had chosen was set, and she had to see it through.

As the trial date approached, Monie steeled herself for the battle ahead. She was no longer the innocent girl who had fallen for Rico's charms. She was a survivor, ready to face the storm and reclaim her life. The streets had shown her their darkest side, but Monie was determined to rise above it and find her way back to the light.

Chapter 6: Decision Time

Monie sat alone in the sterile, dimly lit room, her mind racing. The feds had laid it all out: testify against Rico and possibly save herself, or stay loyal and face a decade behind bars. Her heart was a battlefield of conflicting emotions—love for Rico, fear for her future, and the weight of the impossible decision she had to make.

The door creaked open, and Rico was escorted in, his hands cuffed. The agents left them alone, but the tension in the room was suffocating.

"Monie, baby, you gotta listen to me," Rico said, his voice urgent and pleading. "You can't trust them. They'll screw you over just to get what they want."

Monie looked at him, her eyes filled with tears. "Rico, they said I could go to prison for ten years. I don't know if I can do that."

Rico's eyes softened, and he tried to reach for her, but the cuffs held him back. "I know it's scary, but you gotta stay strong. We'll get through this together. I promise you."

"How, Rico? How are we supposed to get through this?" Monie's voice cracked, her fear and frustration bubbling over. "You lied to me. You put me in danger without even telling me the truth."

"I'm sorry, Monie. I never wanted this for you. I was tryin' to keep you safe, keep you out of it," Rico said, desperation in his eyes. "But if you testify, it's over for both of us. They'll throw me away for life, and you'll be lookin' over your shoulder forever."

Monie shook her head, the tears flowing freely now. "I don't know what to do, Rico. I love you, but I'm scared."

"Don't let them break us, baby. Stay silent, and we'll find a way. Trust me," Rico pleaded, his voice cracking with emotion.

The agents returned and led Rico away, leaving Monie alone with her thoughts once more. She felt like she was drowning, each breath a struggle. She needed advice, needed to hear from the people who truly cared about her.

Later that day, Monie's family was allowed to visit her. Her mother and brother, Jamal, sat across from her, their faces etched with worry and fear.

"Monie, baby, you have to think about your future," her mother said, reaching out to hold her hand. "We can't lose you to this mess."

"Ma, I love him. But this is all so much," Monie whispered, her voice trembling.

Jamal leaned forward, his expression stern but caring. "Sis, Rico got you into this. You gotta save yourself now. He made his choices, and now you have to make yours."

"I feel like I'm betraying him," Monie said, tears streaming down her face.

"You're not betraying him. You're saving your life," Jamal said firmly. "Think about it. Ten years in prison or a chance to start over. Don't let his mistakes ruin your life."

Monie's mother squeezed her hand tightly. "We'll support you no matter what. But please, think about what's best for you. We can't bear to see you suffer."

The pressure from all sides was overwhelming. Monie felt like she was being torn apart, each piece of advice pulling her in a different direction. She loved Rico deeply, but the fear of losing everything she had worked for was crippling.

That night, alone in her cell, Monie replayed everyone's words in her mind. Rico's desperate pleas, her family's heartfelt advice, and the cold, hard reality of the feds' offer. She lay awake, staring at the ceiling, knowing that whatever decision she made would change her life forever.

Morning came, and with it, a sense of grim determination. Monie knew what she had to do, even if it broke her heart. She couldn't let herself be dragged down by Rico's choices. She had to think about her future, her freedom.

When the agents came for her, she stood tall, her heart heavy but her resolve firm. "I'll testify," she said, her voice steady despite the turmoil inside.

The agents nodded, leading her away to prepare for what lay ahead. Monie's decision was made, and there was no turning back. The path to her freedom was fraught with pain and betrayal, but she knew it was the only way to save herself. As she walked down the cold, gray hallways, Monie whispered a silent prayer, hoping for the strength to face the storm and emerge on the other side.

Chapter 7: In Too Deep

Monie's decision to testify against Rico set off a chain reaction that she could never have anticipated. The once supportive community now turned its back on her. Whispers followed her everywhere she went, and the eyes that used to greet her with warmth now only held judgment and suspicion. The weight of being labeled a snitch was unbearable, and Monie felt the walls closing in.

At work, things were no better. She had always been a rising star at the marketing firm, but now, her colleagues avoided her, and her boss started finding fault in everything she did. It wasn't long before she was called into the office.

"Monie, we've appreciated your contributions here, but given the recent developments, we feel it's best for both parties if we part ways," her boss said, avoiding eye contact.

"You're firing me because I'm trying to save myself?" Monie's voice was barely above a whisper, a mix of shock and hurt.

"It's not personal, Monie. It's just business," he replied, but the words felt like a knife to her heart.

Leaving the office for the last time, Monie felt like she was walking through a nightmare. Her dreams, her ambitions—everything was slipping away. The stress was overwhelming, and she could feel it taking a toll on her body. Sleepless nights led to dark circles under her eyes, and the constant anxiety left her feeling like a shell of her former self.

One evening, she sat alone in her apartment, staring blankly at the television. The room felt too big, too empty. She barely noticed her phone buzzing until the fourth ring.

"Monie, it's Rico," the voice on the other end said, low and urgent.

"Rico, I told you we can't talk," Monie replied, her voice strained with exhaustion.

"Listen to me, baby. You gotta help me. They're closing in on me. We need to get our stories straight," Rico said, his tone shifting from desperate to manipulative.

"Rico, I can't do this anymore. I lost my job, the community hates me, and I'm falling apart," Monie cried, the tears finally breaking free.

"Baby, you knew what you were getting into when you decided to snitch. Now you gotta deal with it," Rico snapped, the harshness in his voice catching her off guard.

"Are you serious? I did this because you lied to me, because you put me in danger!" Monie shouted back, her anger bubbling over.

"You think you're the only one suffering? I'm facing life in prison, Monie! And you're over there whining about losing a damn job?" Rico's voice was venomous, revealing a side of him Monie had never seen before.

"Rico, you're the one who dragged me into this mess. Don't you dare put this on me," Monie retorted, her voice shaking with a mix of anger and fear.

"Fine. Do what you gotta do, but remember this, Monie. If I go down, I'm taking you with me," Rico said, hanging up the phone with a finality that left Monie trembling.

She sat there in stunned silence, the words echoing in her mind. The man she thought she loved, the man she thought she was protecting, had just shown his true colors. Rico wasn't the charming protector she had fallen for—he was a manipulative, desperate criminal willing to do anything to save himself.

The realization hit her like a tidal wave. Monie was in too deep, and the only way out was to see this through. But the cost was high. Her mental health was deteriorating, her physical health was suffering, and the people she once called friends now saw her as a pariah.

In the days that followed, Monie withdrew even more. She barely left her apartment, the once vibrant young woman now a ghost of her former self. The stress and fear consumed her, and she struggled to find any semblance of hope.

But in the quiet moments, when the noise of the outside world faded, Monie found a flicker of resilience. She had made her choice to survive, and now she had to find the strength to endure. The streets had shown her their darkest side, but she was determined to rise above it. Monie knew the road ahead would be fraught with challenges, but she was ready to face them, one step at a time.

Chapter 8: Friends and Foes

Monie felt like she was walking through a minefield. The whispers followed her wherever she went, the accusing eyes of her once-friendly neighbors now filled with distrust. Her old friends had either vanished or were circling like vultures, trying to see what they could get out of her crumbling world.

One afternoon, Monie ran into Keisha at the corner store. Keisha, who used to be her closest confidante, barely looked at her.

"Keisha, can we talk?" Monie asked, her voice barely above a whisper.

Keisha glanced around, clearly uncomfortable. "I don't know, Monie. People talkin' 'bout you. They sayin' you snitched on Rico."

"I had no choice. You know I didn't want this," Monie pleaded, her eyes searching Keisha's for a hint of their old bond.

Keisha sighed, shaking her head. "I gotta go. Take care, Monie." And just like that, she was gone, leaving Monie standing alone, the cold reality of her isolation sinking in deeper.

Back home, Monie's phone buzzed with a text from an unknown number: "Need to talk. Meet me at the old warehouse tonight. -T"

Monie's heart raced. Who was reaching out to her, and why? She was desperate for any semblance of support, so she decided to take the risk.

That evening, Monie slipped into the shadows of the old warehouse district, her nerves on edge. She spotted a figure standing by the entrance, their face obscured by a hood. As she approached, the person lifted their head, revealing a familiar face—Tyrone, one of Rico's former associates.

"Tyrone? What are you doing here?" Monie asked, her voice shaking.

"Relax, Monie. I ain't here to hurt you," Tyrone said, his voice low and calm. "I heard 'bout what happened with Rico. Figured you might need some help."

Monie narrowed her eyes, suspicion creeping in. "Why would you help me? You were tight with Rico."

Tyrone smirked, shaking his head. "That's what he wanted you to think. Rico screwed a lot of us over, used us for his own gain. You ain't the only one he lied to."

Monie felt a flicker of hope. "So what now? How can you help me?"

"Rico's got enemies, Monie. People who want him gone. We can help each other. I got connections, info that could be useful to you and the feds," Tyrone explained, his tone serious.

Monie hesitated. Trusting Tyrone was a gamble, but she was running out of options. "What do you want in return?"

Tyrone shrugged. "Just a chance to take Rico down. He's done too much damage. We both need to make sure he pays."

As Monie left the warehouse, her mind raced with possibilities. Tyrone's offer was risky, but it might be the lifeline she needed. Back home, she replayed their conversation, wondering if she could really trust him.

The next day, Monie's doorbell rang. She opened it to find Lisa, another old friend, standing there with a fake smile plastered on her face.

"Monie, girl, I heard 'bout your situation. Just wanted to check on you," Lisa said, stepping inside uninvited.

Monie could see through Lisa's act. "What do you want, Lisa? Why are you really here?"

Lisa's smile faltered, and she glanced around nervously. "Look, I'm just trying to help. Maybe we can, you know, work something out. You must have some dirt on Rico. Might be worth something."

Monie's anger flared. "Get out, Lisa. I don't need fake friends trying to use me."

Lisa's face twisted with anger. "Fine. But don't come crying to me when you're all alone."

As the door slammed behind Lisa, Monie felt a surge of resolve. She couldn't rely on her old friends—they were either scared or looking to exploit her situation. But maybe, just maybe, she could find allies in unexpected places.

Days turned into weeks, and the gossip in the streets only grew louder. People whispered about Monie's deal with the feds, about Rico's downfall, and the power vacuum it created. The betrayal and chaos in the streets made Monie's life even more precarious.

Monie met with Tyrone regularly, exchanging information and planning their next moves. She began to see the cracks in Rico's empire and the true extent of his manipulation. Rico was getting desperate, making mistakes, and Monie knew their time was running out.

One night, Monie received a message from Tyrone: "Got something big. Meet me ASAP."

She hurried to their usual spot, her heart pounding. Tyrone was already there, his expression grim. "Rico's planning something, a big move to take you out before the trial. We need to act fast."

Monie's blood ran cold. The danger was escalating, and the stakes were higher than ever. She looked at Tyrone, determination in her eyes. "Let's do this. It's time to end it."

The streets were closing in, but Monie was ready to fight back. With unexpected allies by her side and a new sense of purpose, she was determined to survive the chaos and betrayal. The final showdown was coming, and Monie was prepared to face it head-on, no matter the cost.

Chapter 9: Legal Struggles

Monie's world had become a whirlwind of legal battles and mounting pressure. Her lawyer, Mrs. Jenkins, was a seasoned professional who had seen it all, but even she seemed overwhelmed by the mountain of evidence stacked against Monie.

"Monie, we have a lot of work to do," Mrs. Jenkins said, her voice firm but kind. They sat in a small, cluttered office, the air thick with tension.

"I know, Mrs. Jenkins. I just don't understand how it got this bad," Monie replied, her voice shaking. She felt like she was drowning, each piece of evidence a stone pulling her further under.

Mrs. Jenkins spread out the files on the desk. "They've got recordings, transactions, witness testimonies... It's not looking good. But we have to stay focused. Our best bet is to prove you were unaware of Rico's activities and that you were coerced."

Monie nodded, trying to absorb the gravity of her situation. Every day was a new struggle, and the reality of a long prison sentence loomed over her like a dark cloud. Pre-trial hearings were grueling, each session a reminder of how deep she was in this mess.

The courtroom was a cold, sterile place, filled with people who seemed determined to see her fail. The judge, the prosecutors, even the audience—all eyes were on her, and she could feel their judgment. Monie's heart pounded in her chest as she took her seat next to Mrs. Jenkins.

The prosecutor, Mr. Wallace, was ruthless. "Your Honor, we have substantial evidence linking Ms. Williams to Mr. Hernandez's criminal activities. The recordings alone are damning."

Mrs. Jenkins stood, her expression resolute. "Your Honor, my client was unaware of Mr. Hernandez's operations. She was manipulated and coerced. We intend to prove her innocence."

The judge nodded, but Monie could see the skepticism in his eyes. She felt a sinking dread as the hearing continued, each piece of evidence presented like a nail in her coffin.

After the hearing, Monie and Mrs. Jenkins sat in a small conference room. "Monie, we have to prepare for the worst. The feds are pushing hard for your testimony. They want Rico, and they see you as the key to getting him."

"I know. But what if I testify and they still lock me up? What if Rico finds a way to get to me?" Monie's voice trembled, the fear in her eyes unmistakable.

Mrs. Jenkins sighed. "It's a risk, but it's your best shot. We can try to negotiate a better deal, but you have to be willing to cooperate fully."

The pressure was mounting, and Monie felt like she was being crushed under its weight. Every day, the feds pushed harder, demanding more information, more cooperation. They visited her regularly, their questions relentless and unforgiving.

"Monie, we need you to testify against Rico. You're our best chance at taking him down," Agent Rodriguez said, his tone insistent.

"I'm scared. You don't understand what he's capable of," Monie replied, her voice barely above a whisper.

"We'll protect you. Witness protection, new identity, whatever it takes. But you have to help us," Agent Rodriguez pressed.

Monie felt trapped. The walls were closing in, and the reality of her situation was inescapable. Her life was falling apart, and every choice seemed to lead to more danger. She had to decide whether to take the deal and risk Rico's wrath or stay silent and face a long prison sentence.

The sleepless nights and constant anxiety were taking a toll on her mental and physical health. She felt weak, exhausted, and utterly alone. The once vibrant, confident woman she had been was now a shadow of her former self, beaten down by the relentless pressure.

One evening, Monie sat alone in her apartment, staring blankly at the documents spread out before her. Her phone buzzed with a text from Tyrone: "We need to meet. Got some info that might help."

She agreed, desperate for any lifeline. They met at their usual spot, and Tyrone looked more serious than ever. "Monie, I found something. Rico's got dirt on the feds. If we can get our hands on it, we might be able to cut a deal."

Monie's eyes widened. "Are you serious? This could change everything."

"It's risky, but it's our best shot," Tyrone said, his voice grim.

As Monie left the meeting, she felt a flicker of hope. The road ahead was still treacherous, but she had a chance—however slim—to turn things around. The legal battles were far from over, and the stakes were higher than ever. But Monie was determined to fight, to claw her way out of the darkness and reclaim her life.

The streets had taught her to be tough, but now, the courtroom was her battleground. And Monie was ready to face the fight of her life.

Chapter 10: The Snitch Dilemma

Monie sat at her kitchen table, staring at her phone, contemplating her next move. She needed to talk to someone she could trust, someone who wouldn't judge her. She dialed Keisha's number, hoping her friend would pick up this time.

"Keisha, it's Monie. Can we talk?" she asked, her voice barely above a whisper.

"Monie, girl, what's goin' on? You sound stressed," Keisha replied, her tone softer than it had been in weeks.

"I need to see you. Can you come over?" Monie pleaded, the desperation clear in her voice.

"Yeah, I'll be there in a bit," Keisha said, hanging up.

Half an hour later, Keisha was sitting across from Monie, her eyes filled with concern. "Alright, spill. What's got you so worked up?"

Monie took a deep breath, her hands trembling. "The feds want me to testify against Rico. If I don't, I could go to prison for ten years."

Keisha's eyes widened. "Damn, Monie. That's serious. What you gonna do?"

"I don't know. I love Rico, but he lied to me, put me in danger. And now his people are threatening me, telling me to stay loyal," Monie said, her voice shaking.

Keisha leaned forward, her expression intense. "What kind of threats?"

"Calls, texts, even a note on my car. They're saying if I snitch, they'll come for me," Monie explained, tears welling up in her eyes.

Keisha sighed, shaking her head. "You gotta do what's best for you, Monie. Rico ain't worth your life. You gotta think about your future."

"I know, but it's not that simple. I'm scared, Keisha. And I don't want to betray him," Monie admitted, her voice cracking.

"Look, if Rico really cared about you, he wouldn't have put you in this position. You gotta protect yourself," Keisha said firmly.

Just then, Monie's phone buzzed with a message. She glanced at the screen and froze. It was another threat, this time more explicit. "Stay loyal, bitch, or you'll regret it."

Keisha saw the message and her face hardened. "This is serious, Monie. You can't ignore this. You need to tell the feds."

Monie nodded, the fear in her eyes giving way to determination. "You're right. I need to do what's best for me."

A few days later, Monie was sitting in a café, waiting for Tyrone. He had some information that might help her case, and she was desperate for any advantage. When he arrived, he slid into the seat across from her, his expression serious.

"I found out somethin' 'bout Rico. He's been seein' other women, got a few baby mamas he never told you about," Tyrone said, his voice low.

Monie's heart sank. "What? Are you sure?"

"Yeah. I got proof," Tyrone replied, handing her a folder. Inside were photos, texts, and documents detailing Rico's affairs and children.

Monie's hands shook as she looked through the evidence. Rico's betrayal cut deep, adding another layer of pain to her already shattered heart. "I can't believe this. He lied about everything."

"Monie, you gotta use this. The feds will eat this up. It shows how dirty he really is," Tyrone said, his tone insistent.

Monie nodded, her resolve hardening. "You're right. This changes everything."

That night, Monie sat alone in her apartment, the weight of her decision pressing down on her. She loved Rico, but he had deceived her, endangered her, and now she knew he had been unfaithful too. The threats from his associates only fueled her determination to protect herself.

Monie picked up her phone and called Agent Rodriguez. "I'll testify," she said, her voice steady. "I have more information for you."

The next morning, Monie met with the feds, handing over the evidence Tyrone had given her. Agent Rodriguez looked through it, nodding with satisfaction. "This is good, Monie. It strengthens your case and helps us take Rico down."

Monie felt a mix of relief and sorrow. She had made her choice, and there was no turning back. The road ahead was still fraught with danger, but she knew she had to see it through. Rico's betrayal had given her the final push she needed to fight for her own survival.

As she left the federal building, Monie felt a weight lift off her shoulders. The decision had been agonizing, but she knew it was the right one. She had chosen to protect herself, to fight for her future, and to break free from the chains of Rico's lies and manipulation. The path ahead was uncertain, but Monie was ready to face whatever came next, determined to reclaim her life and find a way out of the darkness.

Chapter 11: Breaking Point

Monie sat in her car, parked outside her apartment, trying to calm her racing heart. The day had been long, and the weight of her decision to testify against Rico pressed heavily on her shoulders. She took a deep breath, steeling herself to face another night of anxiety and fear. As she stepped out of the car, she noticed a shadowy figure lingering near the entrance.

"Yo, Monie," the figure called out, stepping into the dim light. It was Darnell, one of Rico's rivals. He had a reputation for being ruthless and unforgiving.

"What do you want, Darnell?" Monie asked, her voice trembling despite her attempts to sound brave.

Darnell smirked, his eyes glinting with malice. "Just wanted to have a little chat. Heard you been talkin' to the feds."

"That's none of your business," Monie snapped, trying to push past him.

Darnell grabbed her arm, his grip painfully tight. "Oh, it's my business, alright. Rico's going down, and if you don't watch yourself, you're goin' down with him."

Monie tried to wrench her arm free, but Darnell was too strong. "Let go of me!" she shouted, panic rising in her chest.

"Listen here, bitch," Darnell hissed, leaning in close. "You think Rico can protect you? Think again. You're on your own out here."

With a sudden burst of strength, Monie shoved Darnell away, her adrenaline spiking. "I'm not scared of you," she lied, her voice shaking.

Darnell laughed, a cold, chilling sound. "You should be. This ain't over, Monie. Not by a long shot." He released her and walked away, leaving Monie standing there, trembling and on the verge of tears.

Monie hurried inside, locking the door behind her. Her hands shook as she dialed Agent Rodriguez's number. "I need to talk to you. Now," she said, her voice barely steady.

An hour later, Monie sat in the familiar, cold conference room at the federal building. Agent Rodriguez entered, his expression serious. "What happened, Monie?"

"Darnell. He threatened me. Said I'm on my own and Rico can't protect me," Monie explained, her voice breaking.

Agent Rodriguez nodded, leaning forward. "Monie, this just proves what we've been telling you. You're not safe as long as you're involved with Rico. You need to cooperate fully with us."

Monie's resolve hardened. "I'm done with Rico. I'll testify. Whatever it takes to protect myself."

The agent smiled slightly, relief evident on his face. "You're making the right choice, Monie. We'll make sure you're safe. But we need you to be completely honest with us, hold nothing back."

Monie nodded, feeling a strange sense of calm settle over her. "I will. I'm ready."

Over the next few days, Monie met with the feds repeatedly, going over every detail of her time with Rico. She told them everything—his deals, his associates, the threats she'd received. The more she talked, the lighter she felt, as if a heavy burden was slowly lifting.

But the nights were still filled with fear. Every noise, every shadow outside her window made her jump. The streets were dangerous, and Monie knew she had made powerful enemies. She had to stay strong, keep her focus on the end goal—her freedom.

The day of her testimony approached quickly. Monie stood in front of the mirror, taking a deep breath. She had traded her usual streetwear for a conservative outfit, hoping to present herself as credible and trustworthy. The transformation felt strange, but necessary.

As she walked into the courtroom, the eyes of the jury, the judge, and the spectators all turned to her. She could feel their scrutiny, their judgment. But Monie held her head high, determined to see this through.

Rico sat at the defendant's table, his gaze burning into her. He looked more desperate than she had ever seen him, his once confident demeanor shattered. Monie felt a pang of sadness, but she pushed it aside. This was about her survival, her chance to reclaim her life.

Agent Rodriguez stood by her side as she took the stand. "Do you swear to tell the truth, the whole truth, and nothing but the truth?" the bailiff asked.

"I do," Monie replied, her voice clear and unwavering.

As she began her testimony, recounting the events that had led her here, Monie felt a strange sense of empowerment. She was taking control of her fate, standing up against the man who had manipulated and endangered her. The fear was still there, but it was overshadowed by her determination to break free.

The courtroom was silent as Monie spoke, every word a step closer to her freedom. She could see the impact her testimony had on the jury, the prosecutors, even Rico. The truth was finally coming to light, and Monie was no longer a pawn in Rico's game.

As the day drew to a close, Monie felt a sense of relief wash over her. The road ahead was still uncertain, but she had taken the first step towards a new life. She had faced her breaking point and come out stronger. Now, she was ready to fight for her future, no matter what it took.

Chapter 12: Testimony and Betrayal

The courtroom was packed, buzzing with the hum of murmured conversations and the click of cameras. Rico's trial had become a media spectacle, drawing attention from all corners of the city. Monie sat in a small room off to the side, waiting for her turn to take the stand. Her heart pounded in her chest, each beat a reminder of the gravity of what she was about to do.

Agent Rodriguez entered, giving her a reassuring nod. "You ready, Monie? It's time."

Monie took a deep breath and nodded. "Yeah, I'm ready."

As she walked into the courtroom, all eyes turned to her. The whispers grew louder, a chorus of judgment and curiosity. She could feel the weight of their stares, the scrutiny piercing through her. Rico sat at the defense table, his eyes fixed on her with a mixture of anger and betrayal.

Monie took the stand, the bailiff swearing her in. "Do you swear to tell the truth, the whole truth, and nothing but the truth?"

"I do," she replied, her voice steady despite the storm raging inside her.

The prosecutor approached, a confident smile on his face. "Ms. Williams, can you please recount your relationship with Rico Hernandez and your knowledge of his criminal activities?"

Monie took a deep breath, her mind flashing back to the moments that had led her here. She began to speak, her voice clear and unwavering, recounting everything—the late-night meetings, the whispered phone calls, the stash of drugs and money she had found. She painted a vivid picture of Rico's criminal empire, exposing every detail.

The courtroom was silent, every word she spoke hanging in the air like a weight. She could see the reactions in the jury's eyes, the shock, the disbelief, and the slow dawning realization of the truth.

As Monie continued, she felt a strange sense of empowerment. She was no longer a victim, no longer trapped in Rico's web of lies. She was taking control, reclaiming her life, and bringing the truth to light.

The defense attorney tried to discredit her, questioning her motives and loyalty. "Ms. Williams, isn't it true that you only agreed to testify to save yourself from prison?"

Monie met his gaze, her eyes steady. "Yes, I agreed to testify to save myself. But that doesn't change the fact that everything I've said is true. Rico Hernandez is a criminal, and he needs to be held accountable."

The attorney pressed on, but Monie held her ground, refusing to be intimidated. She had come too far to back down now.

When her testimony was finally over, Monie stepped down from the stand, feeling a mix of relief and exhaustion. She returned to her seat, the weight of the courtroom's gaze still heavy on her shoulders.

The trial continued, but Monie's testimony had set the tone. The evidence was damning, and the prosecution used every word she had spoken to build their case. The media latched onto the story, painting Monie as both a hero and a traitor. The headlines were ruthless: "Girlfriend Turned Snitch Brings Down Crime Boss" and "Love and Betrayal in the Streets."

Rico's conviction was swift. The jury found him guilty on all counts, and he was sentenced to life in prison without the possibility of parole. The courtroom erupted in chaos, reporters clamoring for statements, the public divided in their opinions.

Monie walked out of the courtroom, feeling a strange mix of triumph and loneliness. She had done what she needed to do, but the cost was high. The streets buzzed with gossip, and she knew that her betrayal had made her a target.

As she left the courthouse, a crowd of reporters swarmed her. "Monie, how do you feel about the verdict?" "Do you regret testifying against Rico?" "What's next for you?"

Monie kept her head down, pushing through the throng of people. She had no answers for them, only the knowledge that she had done what she had to do.

In the days that followed, Monie found herself isolated. Friends she had once trusted now kept their distance, fearful of the backlash. The community that had once embraced her now viewed her with suspicion and disdain. She was alone, left to navigate the dangerous aftermath of her decision.

The threats didn't stop. Rico's associates, now leaderless and angry, directed their fury at Monie. She received ominous messages, saw shadowy figures lingering near her apartment, and felt the constant pressure of being watched.

Monie's life had changed irrevocably. She had exposed Rico's criminal empire, but in doing so, she had also exposed herself to the harsh realities of betrayal and survival. The streets were unforgiving, and Monie knew that she had to stay vigilant, always looking over her shoulder.

Despite the fear and isolation, Monie felt a sense of resolve. She had faced her fears, stood up against the darkness, and survived. The path ahead was uncertain, but she was determined to keep moving forward, to find a way out of the shadows and into a future of her own making.

Chapter 13: Aftermath

Monie stood at the window of her small apartment, watching the world outside through a haze of fear and anxiety. The streets, once a vibrant part of her life, now seemed hostile and dangerous. She had taken down Rico, but in doing so, she had painted a target on her back. The label of "snitch" hung over her like a dark cloud, and every day felt like a battle for survival.

The harassment started almost immediately after Rico's conviction. People she once called friends now crossed the street to avoid her. Strangers whispered as she passed, their eyes filled with contempt. It wasn't long before the threats began—messages scrawled on her door, anonymous phone calls in the dead of night.

"Snitches get stitches," one note had read, taped to her car window.

Monie ripped it off, her hands shaking. She was tired of being scared, but the constant pressure was wearing her down. She avoided going out unless absolutely necessary, always looking over her shoulder, never feeling truly safe.

One evening, as she was returning from the grocery store, a group of teenagers blocked her path. Their faces were hard, eyes filled with a mix of curiosity and disdain.

"Yo, you that snitch, ain't you?" one of them sneered, stepping forward.

Monie kept her head down, trying to push past them. "I don't want any trouble."

"Too late for that," another kid said, shoving her hard.

Monie stumbled but managed to keep her footing. She felt a surge of anger. "Leave me alone!"

The teenagers laughed, but one of them, a girl with braids, looked at Monie with a flicker of pity. "Come on, y'all, let's go. She ain't worth it."

Monie watched them leave, her heart pounding. She knew she couldn't keep living like this, always on edge, always afraid. She needed help, someone to talk to, someone who could help her make sense of the chaos her life had become.

The next day, Monie found herself sitting in a small, cozy office, the walls adorned with calming artwork. Across from her sat Dr. Harris, a therapist with kind eyes and a gentle demeanor.

"Monie, it's good to meet you. I understand you've been through a lot," Dr. Harris said, her voice soothing.

Monie nodded, feeling a lump in her throat. "I don't even know where to start."

"Start wherever you feel comfortable," Dr. Harris encouraged.

Monie took a deep breath and began to speak, recounting the events that had turned her life upside down. She talked about Rico, the trial, the threats, and the isolation. The words poured out of her, a torrent of pain and fear that she had been holding back for too long.

Dr. Harris listened patiently, nodding occasionally. "It sounds like you've been carrying a heavy burden, Monie. It's important to acknowledge that what you did took a lot of courage, even if it doesn't feel that way right now."

Monie wiped away a tear. "I just feel so alone. Everyone hates me, and I don't know how to move forward."

"Rebuilding your life won't be easy, but it's possible. It starts with small steps. Finding a support system, setting goals, and most importantly, forgiving yourself," Dr. Harris said gently.

Monie spent the next few weeks attending therapy sessions regularly. She started to explore the pain and trauma she had endured, learning to process her emotions in a healthy way. Dr. Harris helped her develop coping strategies, and for the first time in a long time, Monie felt a glimmer of hope.

She also took steps to protect herself, moving to a new apartment in a different part of town. It wasn't a perfect solution, but it gave her a sense of security. She changed her phone number, cut ties with toxic people, and focused on creating a safe environment for herself.

Through therapy, Monie began to rebuild her self-worth. She realized that her decision to testify against Rico, while difficult, had been the right one. She had stood up for herself, and that took immense strength. Slowly, she started to believe in herself again.

The streets were still dangerous, and the stigma of being a snitch didn't disappear overnight. Monie knew she would always have to be cautious, but she also knew she couldn't let fear control her life. She had faced her demons and survived, and now it was time to start living again.

One day, as she sat in her therapist's office, Monie smiled for the first time in what felt like forever. "I think I'm finally ready to move forward."

Dr. Harris nodded, a warm smile on her face. "You've come a long way, Monie. Keep believing in yourself. You have the strength to overcome anything."

With those words, Monie felt a renewed sense of purpose. The road ahead would still be challenging, but she was ready to face it head-on. She had been through the fire and come out stronger. Now, it was time to rebuild her life, one step at a time.

Chapter 14: New Beginnings

Monie stepped off the bus and into a city that felt both unfamiliar and full of promise. She had left behind the shadows of her past, determined to carve out a new life for herself. The vibrant sounds of the city surrounded her, a symphony of car horns, distant conversations, and the occasional shout from street vendors. It was chaotic, but it was a chaos that Monie found strangely comforting—a sign of life moving forward.

Her new apartment was modest but clean, a small one-bedroom in a building that seemed to hum with the energy of its diverse occupants. She took a deep breath, letting the fresh start fill her lungs. It was time to move on, to reclaim her life from the ashes of her old one.

Finding a job was her first priority. Monie hit the streets with her resume, determined to find something that would help her regain her independence. After a few days of pounding the pavement, she landed a position as an administrative assistant at a local non-profit organization. It wasn't glamorous, but it was honest work, and it gave her a sense of purpose.

Her new colleagues were friendly and welcoming, and for the first time in months, Monie felt a sense of normalcy. She threw herself into her work, eager to prove herself and build a new reputation. Slowly, the fear and anxiety that had plagued her began to fade, replaced by a cautious optimism.

One evening, after a particularly productive day at work, Monie decided to treat herself to dinner at a nearby café. She found a cozy spot by the window and was soon lost in her thoughts, reflecting on how far she had come. The door chime jingled, and a tall, handsome man walked in, his presence commanding attention.

He scanned the room before his eyes landed on Monie. With a warm smile, he approached her table. "Mind if I join you? Looks like it's pretty busy in here."

Monie hesitated for a moment but then nodded. "Sure, go ahead."

"Thanks," he said, sliding into the seat across from her. "Name's Marcus, by the way."

"Monie," she replied, offering a small smile.

They struck up a conversation, and Monie was surprised at how easy it was to talk to him. Marcus had a calming presence, his voice smooth and reassuring. He was a local entrepreneur, running a small but successful tech startup. Unlike Rico, Marcus exuded stability and kindness, qualities that Monie found herself deeply drawn to.

As the evening progressed, Monie felt a connection she hadn't experienced in a long time. Marcus was attentive, genuinely interested in getting to know her without any pretense or ulterior motives. He didn't pry into her past, respecting her boundaries and letting her share only what she was comfortable with.

Over the next few weeks, Monie and Marcus saw each other more frequently. He took her to his favorite spots around the city, introducing her to new experiences and slowly helping her rebuild her trust in others. Monie felt a warmth growing in her heart, a feeling she had thought lost forever.

One night, after a particularly lovely evening out, Marcus walked Monie back to her apartment. They stood outside her door, the city lights casting a soft glow around them.

"I've had a great time tonight, Monie. You're really something special," Marcus said, his eyes sincere.

Monie felt a blush rise to her cheeks. "Thank you, Marcus. You've made me feel... alive again."

He smiled, taking her hand in his. "That's all I want. To see you happy."

As they said goodnight, Monie felt a sense of hope she hadn't known in years. She had been through hell, but she was finally finding her way back. The new city, the new job, and now, Marcus—they were all parts of her fresh start, pieces of a life she was slowly reclaiming.

Monie knew there would still be challenges ahead. The scars of her past were deep, and the memories of Rico's betrayal would take time to heal. But with each passing day, she felt stronger, more capable of facing whatever came next. She was no longer the scared, uncertain woman who had been caught in Rico's web. She was Monie, a survivor, ready to embrace the future and all its possibilities.

With Marcus by her side and a new life unfolding before her, Monie took a deep breath, feeling a sense of peace she hadn't known in years. She was finally moving forward, one step at a time, toward the happiness and stability she deserved.

Chapter 15: The Final Confrontation

Monie was finally finding her groove in the new city. Her job at the non-profit was fulfilling, her circle of friends was growing, and Marcus had become a steady presence in her life, a source of comfort and stability she'd never known. For the first time in what felt like forever, Monie allowed herself to believe she was free from her past. But fate had other plans.

It was a chilly evening when Monie's world was thrown back into chaos. She was walking home from a dinner date with Marcus when her phone buzzed with a news alert. She glanced at the screen and froze, her blood running cold.

"Breaking News: Convicted Drug Lord Rico Hernandez Escapes from Prison"

Monie's heart pounded as she read the headline over and over. Rico was out. He had escaped, and she knew exactly who he would be coming for. Fear wrapped its icy fingers around her heart, but she couldn't let it paralyze her. She had to act.

"Monie, what's wrong?" Marcus asked, noticing her sudden change in demeanor.

"Rico... he escaped," Monie whispered, her voice trembling.

Marcus' face hardened. "We need to get you somewhere safe, now."

They rushed to Monie's apartment, where Marcus helped her pack a bag with essentials. "We can go to my place. It's more secure," Marcus suggested, but Monie shook her head.

"No, I can't put you in danger. I need to face this on my own."

"Monie, you don't have to do this alone," Marcus insisted, but Monie was resolute.

"This is my fight," she said, her voice firm. "I appreciate everything, Marcus, but I need to handle this."

Marcus reluctantly agreed, giving her a burner phone for emergencies. "Promise me you'll call if you need anything."

"I promise," Monie said, giving him a quick kiss before heading out.

Monie knew Rico well enough to guess his moves. She headed to her old apartment, the one she had left behind. It was a long shot, but something told her Rico would come looking for her there. She parked a few blocks away and approached the building cautiously.

As she neared the entrance, a shadow detached itself from the darkness. Rico. He looked gaunt, his eyes wild with rage and desperation.

"Monie," he growled, his voice dripping with venom. "You thought you could get away from me?"

Monie stood her ground, her heart pounding but her resolve unwavering. "It's over, Rico. You don't control me anymore."

Rico lunged at her, but Monie was ready. She dodged his attack, grabbing a broken piece of pipe from the ground. "Stay back, Rico. I don't want to hurt you."

"Hurt me? You already did," Rico snarled, advancing again.

Monie swung the pipe, catching him in the shoulder. Rico stumbled back, shocked by her ferocity. "You think you can beat me?" he spat.

Monie's voice was steady. "I know I can."

Rico rushed her again, but this time Monie didn't back down. She fought with a strength she didn't know she had, every swing of the pipe fueled by the pain and fear he had caused her.

They struggled, but Monie's determination gave her the upper hand.

Finally, Rico fell to the ground, defeated. Monie stood over him, her breath coming in ragged gasps. "It's over, Rico."

Suddenly, the sound of sirens filled the air. The feds had tracked Rico's escape, and they arrived just in time. Agents swarmed the scene, restraining Rico and leading him away in handcuffs.

Agent Rodriguez approached Monie, his expression one of relief and admiration. "You did good, Monie. You're safe now."

Monie nodded, tears streaming down her face. The nightmare was finally over. Rico was going back to prison, and this time, he wouldn't be getting out. She had faced her worst fears and emerged victorious.

As the agents took Rico away, Monie felt a weight lift off her shoulders. The shadow of her past had finally been vanquished. She was free.

Marcus arrived soon after, pulling Monie into a tight embrace. "You're okay," he whispered, his voice filled with relief.

"I am," Monie replied, feeling a sense of peace she had never known. "It's finally over."

Together, they walked away from the scene, Monie leaning on Marcus for support. She had fought her way through the darkness and come out stronger. Now, she was ready to embrace her new beginning, free from the chains of her past.

Monie took one last look at the apartment, a symbol of the life she had left behind. With a deep breath, she turned her back on it, walking into a future filled with hope and possibility. The streets had tried to break her, but Monie had proven she was unbreakable. And now, nothing could hold her back.

Chapter 16: Healing and Closure

Monie sat on her balcony, watching the sunrise paint the sky in hues of orange and pink. It had been a few weeks since the final confrontation with Rico, and the sense of peace she now felt was both unfamiliar and deeply comforting. The city below was waking up, and for the first time in a long time, Monie felt like she was waking up too.

Her journey of healing had begun in earnest. The nightmares that used to haunt her were becoming less frequent, replaced by dreams of a future filled with hope. Therapy sessions with Dr. Harris continued to be a lifeline, helping her process the trauma and find her inner strength.

"Monie, you've come a long way," Dr. Harris said during one of their sessions. "It's important to acknowledge not just the mistakes, but the resilience you've shown."

Monie nodded, a small smile playing on her lips. "I never thought I'd feel this way again. It's like I'm finally finding myself."

Dr. Harris leaned forward, her eyes warm and encouraging. "That's the beauty of healing. It's not just about moving past the pain, but discovering the strength you had all along."

Monie reflected on those words often. Her journey had been filled with darkness and fear, but she had emerged stronger, more resilient. She no longer felt like a victim; she felt like a survivor.

One evening, Monie sat down with a notebook and pen, deciding it was time to reach out to her family. The past few years had strained those relationships, and she longed to mend the rifts. Her mother and brother, Jamal, had always been her support system, and she needed them now more than ever.

"Hey Ma, it's Monie," she began, her hand shaking slightly as she wrote. "I know things have been rough, and I haven't been the easiest to deal with. But I want to fix things. I miss you and Jamal. Can we talk?"

She sent similar messages to her mother and brother, hoping they would understand. The response was immediate and overwhelmingly positive. They arranged to meet at her mother's house, a place filled with memories of better times.

Walking up to the house, Monie felt a mix of anxiety and anticipation. She knocked on the door, and it swung open almost immediately.

"Monie!" her mother exclaimed, pulling her into a tight hug. "We've missed you so much, baby."

Jamal appeared behind her, his face breaking into a wide grin. "'Bout time you came home, sis."

Monie felt tears prick her eyes as she hugged them both. "I've missed you too. So much."

They sat down in the living room, the familiar surroundings bringing a sense of comfort. Monie took a deep breath and began to share her journey—everything she had been through, the mistakes, the pain, but also the strength she had found.

Her mother listened intently, her eyes filled with tears. "Monie, we've always been proud of you. We just wanted you to be safe. But we're here for you, no matter what."

Jamal nodded, his expression serious. "You're strong, sis. Stronger than you know. And we're with you every step of the way."

Monie felt a weight lift off her shoulders. The love and support of her family were the final pieces she needed to feel whole again. They talked late into the night, laughing, crying, and healing the wounds that had kept them apart.

In the days that followed, Monie found herself embracing her new life with a renewed sense of purpose. She continued her work at the non-profit, finding fulfillment in helping others. Her relationship with Marcus grew stronger, built on a foundation of trust and mutual respect.

One afternoon, as she walked through a park with Marcus, Monie felt a sense of closure. She looked around, taking in the beauty of the world around her, and felt grateful for the journey she had taken. It hadn't been easy, but it had shaped her into the woman she was today—strong, resilient, and unbreakable.

"Monie, you okay?" Marcus asked, noticing her contemplative expression.

Monie smiled, feeling a sense of peace. "Yeah, I'm okay. Better than okay. I'm ready for whatever comes next."

Marcus squeezed her hand, his eyes filled with warmth. "I'm glad to hear that. We've got a bright future ahead of us."

As they walked hand in hand, Monie knew that her past would always be a part of her, but it no longer defined her. She had faced the darkness and emerged into the light, ready to embrace the possibilities of the future.

With her family by her side, a supportive partner, and a renewed sense of self, Monie was ready to write the next chapter of her life. The streets had tried to break her, but she had proven that she was stronger than anything that had come her way. And now, she was ready to live her life on her own terms, free from the shadows of her past.

Chapter 17: Moving Forward

Monie had finally found her footing in her new life. The shadows of her past no longer haunted her every step. The streets that once threatened to consume her were now a distant memory. She had committed to staying away from the dangers that had once lured her in, focusing instead on building a future filled with hope and possibilities.

She threw herself into her work at the non-profit, finding immense satisfaction in helping others navigate the treacherous waters of street life. Her own experiences made her a powerful mentor, and she quickly became a beacon of strength for those seeking a way out. Monie's office was a small, cluttered space, but it was always filled with people looking for guidance and support.

"Monie, I don't know if I can do this," said Jasmine, a young woman who reminded Monie of herself a few years back. "Every time I try to get out, they pull me back in."

Monie leaned forward, her eyes filled with empathy and determination. "Listen, Jasmine, I've been there. I know it feels impossible, but you got more strength than you realize. You just gotta take it one day at a time. Focus on what you want for your future, not what's holding you back."

Jasmine wiped away a tear, nodding. "Thank you, Monie. You give me hope."

Monie smiled, feeling a warmth spread through her. "That's what I'm here for. We'll get through this together."

Monie's dedication didn't go unnoticed. The organization's director, Mr. Johnson, called her into his office one day. "Monie,

I've been watching your work. The way you connect with people, the way you inspire them—it's incredible. We need more people like you."

Monie felt a surge of pride. "Thank you, Mr. Johnson. It means a lot."

"I'd like to offer you a promotion. How would you feel about becoming our new Outreach Coordinator? You'd be in charge of expanding our programs and helping even more people," Mr. Johnson said, his eyes gleaming with admiration.

Monie's heart raced. This was an opportunity to make an even bigger impact. "I'd love that. Thank you for believing in me."

As Monie settled into her new role, she found herself more motivated than ever. She organized workshops, created support groups, and even started a mentorship program for at-risk youth. Her life had come full circle, and she was determined to give back in every way she could.

Her relationship with Marcus continued to flourish. He was her rock, supporting her through every challenge and celebrating every victory. One evening, as they walked along the waterfront, Marcus turned to her, a serious look in his eyes.

"Monie, I've been thinking a lot about us," he began. "You've been through so much, and you've come out stronger than ever. I want to be with you, to support you, and to build a future together."

Monie felt a lump in her throat, her eyes filling with tears of happiness. "Marcus, you've been my anchor. I can't imagine my life without you."

Marcus smiled, pulling her into a tight embrace. "Then let's make it official. Monie, will you marry me?"

Monie gasped, her heart bursting with joy. "Yes, Marcus. Yes!"

The future stretched out before her, filled with hope and endless possibilities. She had found love, stability, and a sense of purpose that she never thought possible.

As Monie stood in front of a group of young women, sharing her story and offering them hope, she realized just how far she had come. The pain and struggles of her past had shaped her, but they didn't define her. She was a survivor, a warrior, and an advocate for change.

"Remember, ladies," Monie said, her voice strong and unwavering. "No matter where you come from or what you've been through, you have the power to change your life. Don't ever let anyone take that away from you."

The room erupted in applause, and Monie felt a deep sense of fulfillment. She had found her calling, and there was no turning back. Her journey was far from over, but she was ready for whatever came next.

Monie looked out at the city, a place that had once been filled with danger and despair but now held promise and potential. She had escaped the shadows, found her light, and was ready to shine it on others.

As the sun set, casting a golden glow over the skyline, Monie whispered a silent thank you to the universe. She was free, she was strong, and she was finally, truly moving forward. The streets had tried to break her, but they had only made her stronger. And now, she was ready to embrace the future with open arms, leaving the darkness behind and stepping into the light.

Don't miss out!

Visit the website below and you can sign up to receive emails whenever Rachael Reed publishes a new book. There's no charge and no obligation.

https://books2read.com/r/B-A-WXARB-UWUOD

BOOKS2READ

Connecting independent readers to independent writers.

Did you love *Codefendant*? Then you should read *Once a Cheater* by Rachael Reed!

Isis, a 31-year-old ride-or-die chick, been holdin' it down for her man Jamal for over a decade. They got a beautiful 4-year-old daughter, and Isis is the perfect girlfriend, workin' a steady job and makin' sure her household is on point. But Jamal? He's for the streets—cheatin', runnin' with shady characters, and blowin' money on other women. Calls from side chicks blow up Isis's phone daily, remindin' her she ain't the only one.

Fed up with Jamal's disrespect and lies, Isis finds herself leanin' on his brother Jowan. He's always there, doin' what Jamal should be doin'. As Jowan steps in more and more, Isis starts feelin' somethin' she ain't felt in a long time—real love and respect. One night, lines get crossed, and they start an affair that's hotter than the summer streets. But things get complicated quick when Isis finds out she's pregnant and ain't sure if the baby is Jamal's or Jowan's.

Jamal's temper explodes when he finds out about their betrayal, and the streets light up with gossip, threats, and danger. Violence erupts, and blood gets spilled. Isis, Jowan, and their tight crew gotta stay ten steps ahead to survive. The game turns deadly, and the stakes get higher with every move they make. In the end, Isis must make the hardest choice of her life—face the deadly consequences of their love or find a way to protect her family from the storm Jamal's rage has unleashed.

Once a Cheater dives deep into the raw, unforgiving streets, where love, loyalty, and betrayal collide. It's a gripping urban drama, packed with twists and turns that'll keep you on the edge of your seat. In this world, survival ain't guaranteed, and trust is a rare commodity. Can Isis and Jowan find their way to a new beginning, or will the streets consume them? Get ready for a wild ride through the dark heart of city life, where every decision can be deadly.

Also by Rachael Reed

Codefendant
Codefendant
Once a Cheater
Once a Cheater
Passport Bro
What Happens in Prison
Preference
Sprinkle Sprinkle
Street Exodus
Street Exodus
Street Royalty